Stories of Unicorns

Rosie Dickins

Illustrated by
Maria Cristina Lo Cascio

Reading consultant: Alison Kelly
Roehampton University

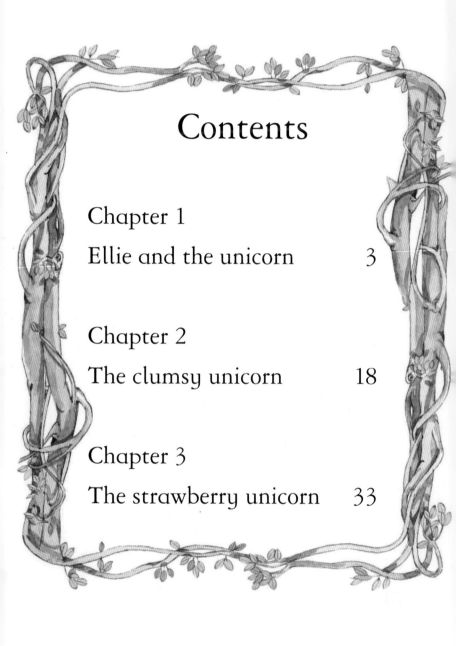

Contents

Chapter 1

Ellie and the unicorn

King Victor was cross. "I want a unicorn!" he roared. But, so far, his soldiers hadn't been able to catch one.

3

"What's stopping you?" he shouted at a soldier. "I know there's a unicorn in the forest!"

"Your majesty," the soldier replied, "it's too clever for us."

Then Lord Malfit had an idea. "Sire," he said, "I hear the kitchen maid, Ellie, has made friends with it. The soldiers could sneak after her and grab it!"

"Well, what are you waiting for?" snapped the King. "And don't come back without my unicorn!"

5

Ellie was in the kitchen, facing a pile of greasy pots. She was thrilled when Lord Malfit gave her the afternoon off.

I'll go and see the unicorn!

It was a hot day, but the
forest was full of shade. Ellie
wandered along, humming.
There were footsteps behind
her, but she didn't hear them.

7

She saw a flash of silver
between the trees.

"The unicorn," Ellie thought
happily, fishing in her pocket
for a sugar lump.

Slowly, the unicorn came closer. It looked at Ellie, then lowered its head to munch the sugar. Ellie stroked its neck. It was like soft, white velvet.

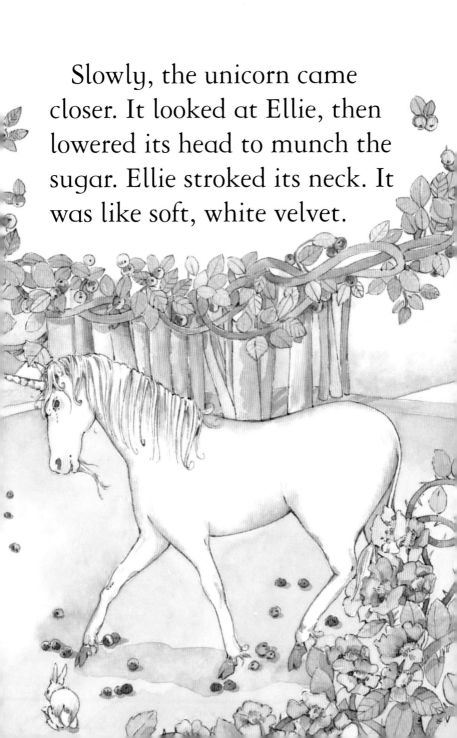

Suddenly, soldiers burst out of the bushes and grabbed the unicorn. It struggled wildly.

"Let him go!" screamed Ellie – but they ignored her. They tied up the unicorn and dragged it away.

The unicorn was hauled into
the King's stable yard. Its hooves
clattered loudly on the stones.

King Victor was overjoyed,
but Ellie was miserable.

"I have to set the unicorn free,"
she decided. "But how can I stop
the soldiers from hearing?"

That night, the palace woke
to an awful racket.

"What's that
noise?" snapped
Lord Malfit.

"G-g-ghosts,"
trembled the King
under the sheets.

"Kitchen thieves!"
screamed the Cook.

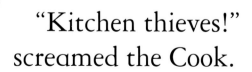

In the kitchen, Ellie was
smashing plates and banging
pans. The din brought the
soldiers running... leaving the
stable yard empty.

13

Ellie grabbed some dishcloths and crept to the stable yard. "I'm getting you out of here," she told the unicorn. It nodded its head gently.

Quickly, she tied the cloths
over the unicorn's hooves.

"Let's go," she whispered,
leading the unicorn across the
yard. Wrapped in cloth, the
hooves didn't make a sound.

15

As they reached the forest, there was a shout. Someone had discovered the empty stable yard. But it was too late.

The next day, King Victor was furious. When Ellie took out the washing, she saw him stomping around the yard.

16

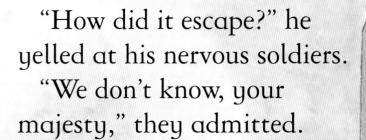

"How did it escape?" he yelled at his nervous soldiers. "We don't know, your majesty," they admitted.

Numbskulls and nincompoops!

Ellie just smiled to herself – and hung up four dishcloths to dry.

17

Chapter 2

The clumsy unicorn

Most unicorns are graceful and elegant. But the unicorn of Fairtree Forest wasn't like most unicorns.

This unicorn was always stumbling over logs...

tangling its tail in bushes...

or catching its horn in branches.

19

And the unicorn was lonely.
It was the only unicorn for
miles around and the other
animals were afraid of it.

If the unicorn looked up at
the birds, they spread their
wings and flew away.

When it lowered its head to say hello to the rabbits, they ran into their burrows.

One day, the unicorn was wandering through the forest when it saw a beautiful butterfly. The unicorn turned to watch it... and tripped over a tree root.

The unicorn struggled, but
it couldn't move its head. Its
horn was stuck in the tree. It
pulled and pulled, but the
horn wouldn't budge.

23

Then the unicorn heard footsteps. A hunter appeared, carrying a sack full of animals. He was whistling and dreaming about food.

When he saw the unicorn, he grinned. "What's this?" he chuckled. "A unicorn, with a horn that's worth its weight in gold!" He lowered his sack and pulled out a knife.

"People pay a fortune for unicorn horns," he muttered. "If I can just cut it off..."

The unicorn was terrified and wrenched at its horn again. In its panic, it pulled even harder.

Suddenly, it stumbled free and tripped over the sack. It tumbled head over heels – and its horn tore the cloth.

Rrrr-rip!

There was a rush of wings and fur, as the animals scrambled out.

27

The hunter was furious to
see his dinner disappear. "Just
wait till I catch you!" he
yelled, waving his knife at the
unicorn. Then he paused.

28

The unicorn was
staring straight at him...
and the hunter no longer liked
the look of its horn. It was
sharp and scary.

29

The hunter's hand shook and
he dropped his knife. "D-don't
hurt me," he stammered and
fled. He never dared hunt in
Fairtree Forest again.

Slowly, timidly, the animals came back and the unicorn tried to make friends. It shook apples from the trees for the rabbits, and tore up the hunter's old sack to make nests.

And from then on, no one
except the hunter was afraid
of the clumsy unicorn.

Chapter 3

The strawberry unicorn

Farmer Jack was very worried about his strawberries. It hadn't rained for days and the plants were starting to droop.

The strawberries needed water, but the well wasn't big enough and the stream had turned into a dirty, bad-smelling trickle.

"I don't know what to do," Jack told his wife, Lily, sadly.

Without water, the plants will die.

"And," he added, "someone's stealing the berries. Soon, we'll have none to sell."

"The thief must be coming while we're asleep," said Lily. "Maybe we can catch him?"

The next day, Jack got up
early. He tiptoed out to the
field – and gasped. There was
a unicorn, right in the middle
of the strawberries.

The unicorn scrambled up,
berries bursting underfoot. It
was covered in juice.

"My goodness, a unicorn,"
cried Jack. "And it's pink!"

The unicorn glanced down
and whinnied crossly.

The unicorn rolled
in the dust, but the
pink didn't come off.

It tried licking
itself – but its
horn got in
the way.

Jack began to feel sorry for
it. "Why don't you come to
the house and have a bath?"
he suggested.

Lily frowned when she saw the unicorn. "So that's our thief," she said.

"Yes," replied Jack, "and it needs a good wash."

"We don't have enough
water," Lily pointed out.

"It can have my bath water,"
said Jack. "I don't mind."

"I do," grumbled Lily. "I'm
the one who has to smell you."
But she picked up the soap.

"If only the stream hadn't gone bad," she sighed, going out to the well. The unicorn pricked up its ears.

Lily hauled up a bucket of water. Then she turned to the unicorn – but it wasn't there.

The unicorn was standing
by the stream. "No, that water
is bad," Lily cried. The unicorn
ignored her and dipped its
horn in the smelly sludge.

42

A trail of clear, sparkling
water rippled out from the
horn, until the whole stream
was running clear and sweet.
"It's a miracle," said Lily.

She ran to get Jack. He was thrilled.

"The strawberries are saved!" he cried. "Unicorns really are magic..."

Now the unicorn stepped into the fresh running water. Jack and Lily rubbed soap all over its coat, until it gleamed silvery white.

The unicorn looked at them
and neighed softly, flicking its
tail happily.

"I think it's saying thank
you," said Lily.

"We're the ones who should say thank you," said Jack. "Maybe we should offer it more berries as a reward?"

But the unicorn made a face and trotted away. "I think it's had enough strawberries to last a lifetime," laughed Lily.

These unicorn stories were inspired by three traditional beliefs. The beliefs are that a unicorn can be tamed by a maiden with a pure heart, that a unicorn can be defeated if its horn gets stuck in a tree, and that a unicorn's horn can purify bad water.

Series editor: Lesley Sims
Designed by Katarina Dragoslavic
Cover design by Russell Punter

First published in 2006 by Usborne Publishing Ltd., Usborne House, 83-85 Saffron Hill, London EC1N 8RT, England. www.usborne.com
Copyright © 2006 Usborne Publishing Ltd.